A Luminous History of the Palm

JESSICA SEQUEIRA

A SUBLUNARY OBJECT

ISBN 978-0-578-64116-4
Library of Congress Control Number: 2020931888

First edition. Third printing.

Manufactured in the United States of America
Printed on acid-free paper
First published by Sublunary Editions in 2020
Design and typesetting by Joshua Rothes

Sublunary Editions
Seattle, WA
sublunaryeditions.com

CONTENTS

A Luminous History of the Palm

I don't know why others write books.

I began to write this book because I love to imagine myself in other lives.

I began to write this book because I was thinking about history.

I began to write this book in search of more luminous associations.

A luminous history seeks to make connections beyond the surface level of great events and statistical data. To do so it takes a symbol, any symbol, as a seed to create anecdotes.

The luminous begins from the small and everyday, the particular and peculiar.

Healer, Yemen

Here I am, on an island that's all rock and dry landscape, mushroom trees, goats wandering over the terrain, turquoise sky. My little bowls are laid before me with broken animal scales, spit from squawking birds that I catch in my nets as they wing past, red resin from spiky palms. The last is the most important, for it goes to make dragon's blood. Dark red pigment smears the rocks and my hands as I crush resin to powder, burn it and mix the ashes with water. For what will I use it? A spell of love? Or one of victory? Suqutra: here white sand piles up on beaches in an alien way, here the cliffs are so steep that they seem inverted. Foreigners think of the island as a strange place, not to be trusted. A place where the unknown happens with unknown effects. Yet despite this, or because of it, they continue to ask for our help. In truth there is nothing strange about us, but perhaps to them, our relationship to nature terrifies by its intimacy. A new request for a healing potion came today. One of the Roman lads broke his leg in a race, and he needs it to be fixed more quickly than if it were left to itself. It is necessary to speak to the cosmos, to ask of it a great favor. Nothing comes for free, of course; sacrifices must be be offered. The potion of dragon's blood will be accompanied by instructions for the appropriate slaughter of an animal. Some work in groups, chanting and sing-ing, but I prefer to work alone, in communion with the great thought. As I carry out my tasks, I remember how vulnerable the human body is, how fragile these spells. How they deal with what can be seen, the fracture, but also with what is deeper than bone.

Sea Captain, Iceland

My mother dreamed of a white ox, killed by a red-flecked ox, avenged by a pure red ox, in its turn avenged by an ox that was the color of sea cattle. She told me this dream with a coy smile that broke into a cackle, as she stoked our fire. Now I shall go into battle armed with such knowledge, which clearly anticipates my death. Fear ceases to be fear when you are clear as to the divine wishes. Old feuds, old conflicts between men over honor, corrected by fate, redeemed by grace: there is nothing new about any of this. It is impossible to resent my mother, however, as the divine put this dream into her head. If I were an Arab, I might have dreamed that a palm tree, the kind which I have never laid eyes upon but of which our voyagers speak, fell over and knocked her into the pot of boiling soup. A different god would have permitted such a thing. But I am not an Arab, and there are no such trees here, and the choppy waves await. I will go forth with valor, behind my sword's ridged blade, to confront the enemy before I fall into the icy waters of the sea.

Warrior, Abbasid Caliphate

Long before we set out, even from the cradle, when dreams of paradise were whispered in our ears as we lay in the laps of our mothers (reams of fabric, moons of faces), we could imagine the seas of green fronds before us, waiting, a radiant path to the utmost radiance. We would come to know it, should we grow up to be courageous, and abiding, and vigorous in our faith. Our dreams were of paradise, and not only of the palms that now meet our blades as we plunge forward, a strong band of men on horses, valiant, holding our banners high, axes at the ready for the coming attack. The trees do not resist; they cede with ease, just as the enemy will soon do. We act in accordance with what is written in Verse 59:5, which states that on the authority of Abdullah, the date palms of Banu Nadir must be cut down and burned; it has been commanded that we must disgrace the rebels. We must uproot their most treasured possession; we must set the fertile alight so that one day we see those palms of which our mothers spoke, awaiting us in the eternal garden. There will be fragrant fountains scented with camphor, and rivers of milk, and shady valleys, and sticky-sweet treats whose wrinkled skins look ugly and hard as leather, but rupture with ease as you bite, to surrender the bliss of their nectar. Illusion: the wisdom of the Creator is such that things are not always as they seem! Now we head back from our task, which was not arduous but simple, for as nobles of Quraish, versed in these arts, to destroy and burn Buwaira and set sparks flying in every direction was mere child's play. Now, exhausted, we are prepared at last for a blazing fire and a hot meal, and the taste of salty roast lamb on our palates. But where is our land? Where are the beloved green forms that always rise from the desert to greet us, serving as our welcome in this great preliminary to paradise? Why are there only charred trunks and mutilated branches, and ash on the ground and the orange fireflies of dying flames, and our mothers howling in pain: 'Sons of our flesh, grieve with us, for the palms in our enemies' land are growing, and we forgot that this land is a mirror. Allah has spoken.'

I began to write this book because I was asking myself questions like these:

What if you were to treat history not as a battlefield, a site of combat, but as a being that you love; what if you were to approach it stroking the tender places behind its ears, speaking to it in low tones, keeping your eyes wide open and looking with trust at its intentions?

What if you were to become conscious of sensitive regions and wounds without poking your fingers into them; what if you were to respond to crises by tracing out a different path along the delicate hairs and veins, the valleys and ridges?

What if you were to hold stories with patience, giving them an encouraging pat; how might they yield up their riches with gratitude? What if you were to lay with them in a Song of Songs, a meadow, a pastoral ideal that treasures both briskness and fragrance, discovering communions of tenderness, forming part of a murmuring brook that alternates between chatter and repose?

What if you were to dance along the breeze as an escape from time's worn paths, babbling your dithyrambs, seeking out movement with rhythm, with joy at last laying a fresh branch of palm between the years?

Apostle, Judea

When Jesus entered Jerusalem, they say that palm branches were waved. Why palms? No one knows for sure. Since the event was unprecedented, his reception may simply have been the default, that is, the same reception that would have been given to a king or hero of war, or even an athlete, as in the Roman tradition champions are honored with palm branches. Or someone may have remembered the lines about the festival described in Leviticus 23:40 and Deuteronomy 16:13–15, which say: 'And you must take for yourselves on the first day the fruit of splendid trees, the fronds of palm trees and the boughs of branchy trees and poplars of the torrent valley, and you must rejoice before Jehovah your God seven days.' Here was Jesus back from exile, not from Egypt it's true, but given the trials that he'd gone through, it might as well have been. A triumphal entry, the scribes write, the beginning of the Passion. The truth is likely a bit more chaotic, as the truth always is. Sure, there was Jesus, atop his donkey, that humble animal which is a symbol of peace, and which appears to have been a happy creature to boot; in all of the paintings, the ass is grinning, pleased to be the center of attention. Following him were the apostles, their gold haloes invisible at the time but there in retrospect. No doubt dozens of spies were slipping through the masses, mentally drafting their reports, but let us focus on the others in the crowd. Draped in cloth of all hues, with faces that alternated between serious, suspicious and gossipy, they were probably less ecstatic at this moment than bewildered at what to do or say, the appropriate way to respond to such a sight. Would it be enough to have the ladies lay out cloth to smooth the way for the donkey's hooves, or ought something more to be done? According to 1 Maccabees 13:51, 'there were harps, and cymbals, and viols, and hymns and songs', but of course many consider this book to be part of the Apocrypha, and it's possible the entrance was largely silent. In the depiction by Pietro Lorenzetti in 1320, most of the people are not even holding palm branches, although some men are scaling palms in the background to cut a few down. All of the preparations seem to be fairly last minute. Maybe palm branches were waved only by a few, since how many palm trees could really have been on hand, how many branches was it truly possible to have cut down with foresight? One imagines that most people in the crowd arrived empty-handed, without prior plans, drawn by the strange sight of this declared prophet atop a donkey—what a sight to tell the grandchildren!—not fully understanding what they were seeing, but all the same awed.

Prince, between Estonia and Russia

They will follow us when we turn, and come after us when we retreat. They will capitalize on what appears to be our surrender, their brash overconfidence lacking the humility that is needed to acknowledge an invisible truth. This will give us victory, if we are able to maintain the strength of our reverence. It is cold, and the ice is slippery; further on, it has begun to crack. You, my Novgorodians, will be at arms with the Teutonic Knights in this bitter cold that stiffens the joints, makes the face blue, bites into the skin, cuts blood flow to the brain and addles the mind. Our enemy is likely already about to succumb, imagining sunny places, palm trees, warm lands, the safe rooms of childhood. This is precisely what you must avoid. As your prince and commander, your dear Prince Nevsky returned from exile, I instruct you, my troops, to do just the opposite. The palm is a chimera, an angel that beckons toward death. The thought of her will make your brain dissociate from your body, so that you will not even care if you die. You must instead tell yourself: 'You may be cold, but this is a fact that you have accepted, and from here it can get no worse.' You must act with full intensity, turning around to surprise them with a counter to their counterattack, plunging forth with shield and lance. If you must keep a face in your mind, let it be the ikon-face of Christ or a saint. The Novgorodian people have placed their trust in us, and we will make good. May the enemy die of its hubris and its dreams of gentle Mediterranean places, far away from this hellish ice. We must find strength in suffering, not avoiding it but accepting its grace without flinching, as like the radiant star above our heads, we remain steadfast.

Rice Farmer, Thailand

Beneath the waters, as we work side by side, your hand reaches toward me often to touch my moist shirt, the cloth around my waist, my skin. Plunged deep, up to our necks, we slice firm stalks with our sickles, we harvest. You press a few grains of rice into my stomach and breasts, and together we laugh at the row of great palm trees which lords over us, without a clue what we're up to. We'd be killed if they knew, you say, and the shadow that falls over your face doesn't come entirely from your sunhat. The trees are watching, always watching. I'm promised to another man, and both of us know it. Yet for now, with only our floating heads visible, it's possible to imagine myself in a red silk pha nung, and you in the chang kben trousers of a prince.

On a recent flight I read a book about contemporary Urdu poetry. The word 'luminous' and its variants repeated again and again. Moin Ahsan Jazbi's anthology Faroa'n *(Luminous)*, *Rajinder Singh Bedi's* Rakhshanda *(also translated as Luminous)*, *Upendar Nath Ashk's* Farzaana *(Resplendent)*, *Salam Machhlishahri's* Angaarey *(Embers)*, *Andaleeb Shadani's* Ek Taabnaak Sitara *(A Luminous Star)*. *My pen burst as I tried to copy them down. The ink bubbled and settled irregularly into the paper, a star, a throbbing palm. It had been days since I'd slept, and crossing through time zone after time zone, all things seemed interconnected.*

Friar, Ireland

When I began to write these annals, my inspiration came from the straightforward accounts of priests in other times, writing on such matters as the black mold that touched the palm trees on their farms, or the number of piglets born to their sows that year. This straightforward account of the good and the bad pleased me, as it gathered all of the divine workings into a single ledger. Thus I embarked on this attempt to record what I have seen for posterity, should there be a posterity. The events of this year have forced me to put greater stock in my journal. No longer is it a mere inventory, for the black mold I must now chronicle is infecting not palm trees, but the skin, the inner organs, the brains of those in my parish. I am just another Franciscan friar, one replaceable member of an eternal order, but I hope that one day the world will wake from this nightmare, and look upon these annals to say: 'God has vanquished evil.' I have visited the ill in Kilkenny; I have made journeys to Dublin where the blackness is even darker; I have read out eulogies for the best of men. This is an evil that attempts to seize control of our earth not through arms or shows of brute physical strength, but by these insidious means, through fever, headache and vomiting, which can lay a man low, swell his parts and in ten days drop him into the coffin. Yet an evil exists that is possibly even greater, which is the response of the spiritual guides. My order is composed of the mendicants who go amongst the poorest men without fear, trusting that God has a great plan which can encompass even this horror. But I see the men of other orders cowering, or retreating to their monasteries to seal up the doors, or giving big sermons to the healthy from a distance, speaking blasphemous phrases about a link between bodily purity and purity of soul, as if the poor sick folk themselves were responsible for their rot. I am leaving a few blank pages now at the end of my book for whoever next takes it up, as I see no end to this. My own death is approaching, I can feel it, thank the heavens from natural causes. Yet this plague will rage on, this blackness that burns through the population and ravages the strength of even the most robust; may I curse a thousand times this black mold that not only afflicts the bodies of men, but strikes black into the souls of those who profit from their deaths.

Mosaic Maker, Italy

We know that we will be remembered as followers and disciples, 'the school of'. Yet we are not bothered. We belong to this period, to the summit of creative activity, and through these great works worldly recognition will come to us. For now we spread stucco, place tiles and fill the gaps between them, before we carefully clean away the excess. There are many panels to fill; the work will take months. God the Father, Mercury, Moon, Saturn, Jupiter, Mars, Sun, Venus. We press the tiles together as closely as possible, with almost no space between them; yet each tile subtly differs in its color and angle, and the effect is to create a shimmering gleam around the angel painted by Our Master. In the evening I approach him where he sits, alone in the gloom. He is familiar with my presence; I have approached before with questions, whatever strikes my mind. Another might call these excuses. 'Your ideas about Plato are known to those of us who love you,' I said. 'The palm tree was a Greek symbol representing the recurring nature of time. Would it not be perfect to include it? Why are there no palms in this new work of yours?' Our Master looked at me, and then laughed. 'You come from a part of the country where palms are less strange than here in Florence,' he reminded me. I looked down at my dark skin; of course he was right. 'Anyhow, my dear boy,' he went on, 'would you have me be so obvious? This work made for my patron and friend, the great banker Chigi, is called *Creation of the World*, but everything about the delicately exposed breasts, contorted muscular arms, scythes, swords, birds and bows, suggests not only eroticism but also violence. These, as you know, are the two great linked forces of the world. Do not forget that your brilliant gold tiles are black on the reverse. All of this can be found in the zodiac, which is cyclical; the zodiac itself is the palm.' Our Master winked, and after I had lain for a while in his arms, I went away to look at the stars in the sky, those little tiles of gold. Then to my pallet for healthy rest, for night will soon flip to morning, and there is work to do.

Opera Singer, Germany

Mozart sweeps into our house as he so often does, knocking lightly before my enthusiastic mother ushers him inside with her frivolous chatter. He himself speaks only the expected courtesies, his lips simpering, his look cool and analytical. When he reaches the drawing room, he kisses my sister and myself on our chins, so as not to disturb our painted faces. We are all too aware of his interest in appearances. He is here to check on us, or rather our progress. Last week he left us the songs, and now he wants to hear what we've done with them. All of them think us such talented sisters, and perhaps they are not wrong. My sister, Dorothea, and I, Elizabeth, are always taken as a pair. Mozart, however, has teased out the essential differences between us. He has chosen me to be the jealous woman, the rejected lover and villain, and my sister to be the King of Troy's beautiful daughter, who adores the same enemy prince as I do, but is rewarded with his love. I will be the screaming banshee upon Cretan beaches, covered in palms that look upon me with their patient skeptical gazes, like gods. Why did he give me the role of the scheming woman, and her the triumphant? I know that Mozart did not write the work himself, and that his librettist Giambattista Varesco is responsible. I know that they do not always share views.

Society gossip has it that they argue over Mozart's tendency to cut and change lines, which naturally no writer likes. Still, the roles were Mozart's choice. And he made that comment, with his small arch of a brow, his cryptic irony, that the role of Electra, princess of Argos, is ever so suited to me, while my sister must sing the part of my rival Ilia. What could be the reason? I try to look at Dorothea with neutrality, but objectively speaking, it is simply true that she has a fatter face, frizzier hair and thicker eyebrows. My theory is that Mozart is an intelligent man, with an appreciation of cruelty, and that this is what gives his work complexity. This must be the reason why he chose me to be the villain, rather than the good woman. My sister and I pull out our scores, and our dual soprano voices alternate. I look at Mozart's fingers pressed together and remember he is a young man, only twenty-five. I am ten years older than he is, my sister ten years older than me. Yet nearly aged, it is she who has received the part of the innocent maiden! Let me be jealous, should Mozart will it. Let my envy soar forth in Italian, a far superior language for emotional drama than German, as Mozart turns the page with an idle flick of the finger and my sister flashes a smile his way. No, I will not allow Ilia to have Idamante; she will not be the Queen of Crete. May the palm trees judge me as they will, when I raise my hands stained with blood.

What does it mean to be luminous? To glow from within, one might say. A material glows when it accumulates a certain density of similar entities in repetition.

Human glow: Blood cells in the cheeks that create a blush.

Animal glow: Neon cells that produce phosphorescence, as in the jellyfish.

Cerebral glow: A compactness of ideas, the brain's 'lightbulb' moment.

Linguistic glow: Often called poetry, with the lyric as tightest possible density.

Historical glow: The repetition of a symbol, personally chosen. A microcosm iterated with contextual variations to illuminate larger material. From inside out, and only then from outside in.

Duchess, France

Another uncomfortable dinner. The maid wheels out the tray of dishes to the table. Outside, the sky is the same gray-blue verging on silver as always. A lovely color, but one has to admit that it does incline one to a certain melancholy. What a good thing that there are so many foreign distractions in this room. The 'Duchess of Palms' they call me, because I love these exotic touches. We're all batty about palms, but I suppose I take the coconut cake. Distractions are so necessary. Tonight, for instance; the cutlery clicks on and on, but my husband says nothing, and neither do I. A less decent man would have skipped dinner; a more decent man would have tried to talk it out with me, explain himself, admit that no explanation was possible except to ask forgiveness. But my husband is what he is, a rake in the style most *authentique*. Thank goodness we are nearing the end of the meal. In the depths of the asparagus platter is a scene of foreign nature. I did not always like palms; at first, I thought they lacked class. Why were the French trying to imitate Asia when they ought to imitate a previous and superior version of France? And then I grew so bored, and my husband became so horrible, and decorating served as such an excellent diversion. Chinoiserie began to creep into my tea service, the wood paneling of my dressers and the design of my dishes, not just the one for asparagus, but also in six or seven cup & saucer sets. Fantastic vines with romantic insinuations weave magic into the dining room, and subtle hints at a darker, more tantalizing reality liven up the dense fabrics in the bedroom and salon. My husband looks with disdain at these objects, worthy of prompt dispatch to the jungle. But I am the mistress of the house, lest he forget. Besides, he himself has a taste for the colorful and gaudy, with his elaborately-curled wigs and silk waistcoats of rich sapphire and gold. He is a trussed-up child pretending to be a man, a peacock, *pardieu*. To some extent I can even understand him, since everything here is so bloody dull, so ordered. French trees form such straight lines on the avenues, unlike the ones on my foreign silk pillowcases. And now, of course, everything must go as if he were the most perfect of husbands. No chaos is possible in our social set. I will have to overlook the damned crime. If he'd casually mentioned that he'd killed a man, I'd have been obliged to do the same, pretending not to hear, changing the subject to the evening's menu or an upcoming party. It sounds dire: and yet my mind is free to flit. I see some empty folding screens where I can have designs inlaid. It might even be possible to print palm patterns on my shoes and on the fabric of the divan. Tomorrow I will stick a few feathers in my hair as mock

palm fronds, a wink at the *noix de coco* which push over
my décolletage. This, at least, lies within my ducal right.

Train Driver, South Africa

Glory, the greatest glory, this is what was drummed into my head when I trained to be a Cape Government Railways officer, a glory that I do feel, even if it seems to be a big word. I drive the men who will make our nation wealthy, the ones will build frontier towns and fight necessary battles, who will come back loaded with jewels and gold. Before they would have gone by ox-wagon, but now there's steam, beautiful dark gray steam that blasts from the metal like a powerful cousin to the steam from horses' nostrils. The men are anxious to reach the end of the line, but first it is necessary to pass through much terrain, the whole of the Great Karoo with its crassulas, euphorbias, stapelias and aloes, bristling up from the territory to dizzy those not made of iron. It is a strange land, a land that is all at once so dizzyingly arid that you begin to believe anything is possible. I have begun to see this movement in the eyes of the men: as the dawning of a miracle. Out here, where dinosaurs once lived, we whizz over the fossils. It's a miracle, too, that I am at the wheel, since these trains did not even exist a few years ago, when I qualified as a mechanic. Often, I think of the chance of things: I could well have been on the greener Eastern line, looking at palm trees, leading my men into wars on the frontier. But no, here I am in this broad barren loam, this scorching fire that turns to bitter cold at night inside the unheated train. And then we are through, and it's bliss to see the sheep of Beaufort West, the simple whitewashed houses of De Aar, and at last Kimberley, where the men fall with their picks and shovels upon the Big Hole, to gouge as many diamonds as they can. Already the diamonds are glimmering in their eyes. None of that for me; I will keep driving this train to eternity, my only diamonds the train headlights, the closest I get to palm trees the green scrub of the terrain, the closest to sea salt the constant dust which still shivers in the air long after the huge mountains were blast through by a feat of engineering, for the greater glory of our railways.

Housewife, New Zealand

My husband has gone abroad as a missionary, but here I am, stuck in this sitting room, surrounded by house plants. They are awful, and yet I keep them because in my mind, they are miniature versions of the huge palms that my husband must be seeing now. But truly, they are awful. I open my little paperback and once again study the words which have engraved themselves in my memory: 'For some strange reason that she couldn't explain she hated looking at palms. Nasty foreign things, she called them in her mind. When they were still they drooped, they looked draggled like immense untidy birds, and when they moved, they reminded her always of spiders. Why did they never look just natural and peaceful and shady like English trees? Why were they forever writhing and twisting or standing sullen? It tired her even to think of them, or in fact of anything foreign...' Katherine Mansfield, this is, in her story 'Such a Sweet Old Lady', in the posthumous collection *A Dove's Nest* assembled by her partner in her honor. I have my doubts about Mansfield, about this voice that hovers between babyishness and cruelty. But on this point, on palm trees, she's got to the grain of something. When I feel most anxious, it soothes me to take down this little book and look at these spiteful words, so much rage directed at a plant. It reassures me that my own frustration isn't out of place, that others before me have felt a similar disgust for exotic forms, and a preference for the soothing shade of the domestic. Why did my husband go off like this to India, to help support the spread of the Christian message in the Empire, instead of staying here, or even going into the lost territories of New Zealand, where there is quite enough poverty, drinking, unemployment and all the rest to keep anyone busy? To Londoners, even our Wellington may seem exotic, let alone India, a land where any civilization must be imposed by force. I pray to God, who may or may not be the same one spread by my George through distant lands, to bring home my husband safe and sound, back to the good old beeches, rimus, tawas, matai, ratas, gully ferns, spinifex, pingao, flax, kauri and kohekohe. Dear God, please bring home George so we can walk again over golden beaches, ride the Kapiti Coach and drink wine while admiring the beautiful mountains of the Rimutaka Range. Dear God, in your goodness, may you uproot all those nasty foreign palms...

I was trained to be suspicious of the Enlightenment and its love affair with reason. Luminous history prefers to takes as its premise a playful first move, an arbitrary selection that one can then follow through. Not one that is randomly generated (as in an Oulipo experiment) but one that is felt to be important by the historian herself.

To be luminous is not the same as to be enlightened. Enlightenment comes from the outside and implies progress. To be luminous is to generate affections and affiliations from the heart, belly and bowels of a situation in time, and form part of an organic system that is possibly infinite. It is to avoid abstraction, at least at the start, to prefer the concrete and sensual, the soft light forged by the bodies of stories as they crush together in violence or embrace.

Harvester, Southern Nigeria

We come at night, when it is cool. The palm fruits are heavy, with bristling surfaces that scrape our hands. We toss them down to the others waiting. The work is repetitive and exhausting, for us and for our wives, who trample the fruits to get at their oil, the soul of the fruit. Where does this oil go? Why can't the whites in other lands use something else for their cooking, their candles, their machines? Our hands are callused, our bodies bruised. Sometimes when I am up there, just below the heart of the tree, I whisper to it: 'Sister, I apologize for taking your fruits. Sister, I am sorry that I cannot leave you to ripen what you bear in peace. The men are planning a revolt but you cannot tell anyone, sister. We will make our plans while inside your womb. We do not want anything from you, just as we do not want them to take anything from us. Sister, listen. Soon it will be over, I promise. Some people think that the business of palm oil replaced slaves, but it is not true. The business of palm oil depends on slaves. We harvesters are needed to pick the palm fruits, to climb the trees. Our women on the other hill cook the nuts until they're soft, so that the oil can be extracted. Then they stomp it in vats like wine. The men harvest, the women do the rest. Three hundred pounds of fruit make thirty-six pounds of oil, they tell us. They say that we need to be more productive, that the English are waiting, cash in hand. They say that we are lucky to be here, on an individual smallholding, rather than a big plantation. They say that in those places, there is no talk like this, only the sound of the whip that gives lashings. Above us the moonfruit shines bright in the sky, far away from the people who will buy your fruits, far away too from this interior of the Bight of Benin. We can imagine nothing worse than our fate in these lands. Sister, be patient with us. It will not be long.'

Chef, Lebanon

[tape begins] You ask what I saw, details. The question is no use, nothing can change. Okay, okay, I will speak. But please have mercy. She had long dark hair and a black dress. He had a suit and smoked. She was a singer at the night club. He was a businessman. Her eyes were languorous. His eyes were yearning. It would be a mistake to know me, she said. Let me invite you to dinner, he pressed. It would be a mistake, she repeated. Dinner, he echoed. We brought the courses directly to the lounge for convenience. They began with salads, heart of palm. The soft tubes gave way with grace under their sharp knifes. Imagine if the heart were like this, she said. A tube so bland and white, he picked up her thought. Like the ivory tusk of an elephant, she went on. With the texture of asparagus, he finished. I didn't mean to hear them speak. But the theme interested me. I have made many of these heart of palm salads. Cherry tomatoes, cucumber, herbs, you can mix in anything. Sprinkled with olive oil and pepper they're nice too, just simple like this. Unlike others I do not put in heart of artichoke, that would be too many hearts. Here my salad comes served with garlic purée, olive oil, lime juice and a good cold mezzeh. Only now are these heart of palm salads popular at the big hotels. Before it was turnip pickle with fresh mint. Turnips are easier, firmer, I would carve them into roses. But palm heart has its delights, too; I can chop it into spirals, circles inside circles, funny wheels. Yes, yes, I'm getting to the point. I'm scared, sirs, I don't want to go on, I am no witness. All I know is cooking. Alright, alright, I will go on. If I must. Please have mercy. My husband will find me, she said. Our hearts will not survive without one another, he insisted. My husband found me before and beat me, she confessed. You could still see her throat with the marks, but he said nothing. They clutched each other's hands. I tried to stop listening. The hearts of palms here are mostly grown in Brazil, sometimes Ecuador or Costa Rica. The local population there harvests and exports *palmitos*. Just a few are kept for the local economy, to eat fresh or bake in pies. France is the country that imports the greatest quantity of palm hearts in the world. There they understand romance; they adore *coeurs de palmier*. Yes, yes, I am getting to the point. Please put that down, I am scared. I adore hearts of palm, she said. So do I, he murmured, and lifted one tenderly toward her mouth. They knew about hearts of palm. It impressed me. Solitary palms with a single stem die when the heart is removed, she said. We will be palms with two stems, and will find a way to survive together even if our hearts are cut away, he said. Their hands were still clutched.

It was not the first time they had met here. The light was violet and emerald on the rooftop. Later it turned scarlet. He came, and their hearts were softer than hearts of palm. Never again will I prepare this dish. His knife sliced right through them. Oh please, have mercy, I cannot go on. Oh please, have mercy [tape ends]

Wrestler, China

Sometimes, at the most crucial moment of the fight, when time stops, I think that I could have been a policeman, or a military officer, or a Manchu bannerman guarding the Forbidden City. All of them are compelled by the state to learn the same things that I do, although of course not to such a high degree of training. They are far from experts in the subject. If my father had not been a *shuai jiao* man, if I had not had the techniques of the Beijing style instilled in me from birth, if those medals and photos had not gleamed at me from the walls as comparisons every day of my life, I might well have ended up selling reeking steamed fish from palm leaves in the street, like the father of my betrothed, Jiang Ying Yue. I know that like the reflected moon in her name, she will follow me in whatever I choose to do. Yet this is what I am, and the respect of the whole region for my name keeps me in good standing with her family. Minutes ago, a tuxedoed presenter introduced my opponent and myself to the public, holding up first my arm, and then his. Both of us wear traditional white outfits as dapper as his western wear, one outfit striped in red, the other in blue. When the round began, I found that we are about equal in build. Both of us are slim, so much so you can see the bones that come through our pale skin. But this is a sport that rewards not weight, but angles. The fighting appears to be done with the arms, but in reality, it is done with the mind. The mindless babble of the commentator, who looks like a professor of literature, comes to my ears from somewhere nearby, but I have trained myself to hear it as ambient noise. Pixelated images of flames blaze on the screen over the mat, a meager imitation of the televised wrestling shows from abroad, yet even so, viewers used to foreign styles would get bored watching us. Save for our bright neon trainers, every aspect of our technique is subtle. I think of my beloved in her seat in the stands, daring to display her devotion to me, escaping the stink of her father's palm leaves, looking intently at the circle where my opponent and I are doing turns, arms locked. I will not let her down. There is nothing between my opponent and myself, no special gear or fancy padding. Nothing but strength of intent. I swing to one side, and with swift resolve deal out the emblematic move of this form: a kick.

We draw on technology; we use search tools; information is unavoidable. But these are only resources. To write a luminous history of the palm, we must compose and order the anecdotes ourselves.

The science of modern technology (the creation of the new from raw materials) and the science of regard for the self (the process of reflection on one's body and consciousness in flux) are necessarily in dialogue. Thoughtful action goes with active thought, in a constant ferrying back and forth.

As honey bees we visit the flowers of palms, carrying pollen from one anecdote to another, seeking out nectar and translating it.

Pianist, Egypt

Some people believe in inspiration, and there's nothing wrong with that. But how many of them actually have careers to speak of? Let me tell you, if I were to wait around all day for a golden light to appear in the distance, or an irrepressible joy to ripple through my being, or my feet to experience the sensation of ice skates attached by an angel, I would be warming my seat at a civil service job, or vending falafel and mahshi on the street to teenage punks. These ideas of inspiration are pretty phrases concocted by people who don't actually work, and whose artistry stops there. I don't wait for inspiration; I place more trust in a slightly burnt-tasting, yet highly effective, coffee. My title is ready: *Dance of the Palm Trees*. I'll deliver it next week to the state orchestra. There's a burning pain in my chest that isn't a heart burning with love; I think it may be acid reflux. They say I'm a hack composer, yet they cannot deny that what I create is beautiful. All of the music directors in the city demand my songs. Who cares where they come from? Isn't the finished piece more important than a celestial process? They put their faith in the divine, but as any good Coptic knows, divine and human nature are one. Not only is the human being divine, the divine is also human. Such a simple and terrible thought, yet this is what complete union means. God does not come as inspiration from without, but through the very imperfect form of the human. Let them understand this, next time they look at my bloodshot eyes and hint that I've been overzealous with the tipple! They are the real heretics. What is more, I can bet you that my life is far calmer than theirs. The innermost emotions, the pulsing spirit, the ancient rhythm in my songs does not come from any shining rays sent by Saint Anthony or Pachomius, any whirling skirts that whip up intense emotions in the crowd, any illumination from the kohl-lined eyes of a single night's companion. Rather, I find my satisfaction in a good breakfast, when I tend to eat too much, tell off my wife for overdoing it with the salt and read a few pages in the daily rag about a train crash, a church bombing or some other stupidity. Then I sit down at my bench, prepared to compose. And as I make flicks on the paper to mark out notes running up and down the page, later to be accompanied by wandering strings which elliptically return to an unseen center, I smile, thinking of how my art fits the description of the worst kind of crime: *premeditated*.

Surfer, California

The fresh air always hits you first, the salt brine flavor that is cleaner than if it were completely pure. I've got my shortboard, bright orange, and a new haircut, with a color that's not the typical peroxide blonde but a streaky blue that I'm trying out for the first time. I've never colored my hair before, but it's the '60s, they say, go wild. I've been coming out here every few days this summer, and have got used to the slowed-down rhythm by now, the warmth, the sand, the ritual of preparing the board before walking it out, the cold that hits you before it becomes familiar and you go for another dip, again and again. I prefer the circular method of waxing my board, though others like the front-to-back or criss-cross. Base coat, top coat, now the shortboard is nice and slick. According to the label, the wax is made from the leaves of the *Copernicia prunifera* palm in northeastern Brazil. The waves must be great there, and I hope to get to know them one day, although I doubt that they could be better than the ones here in California. I'll probably check out the beaches close to home first, Steamer Beach or Lower Trestles, even if for now I'll stick with Cardiff Reef. As I head out toward all of those beautiful waves crashing in, I watch a surfer far better than I am careen over the spume and harder white beneath it, just as with such expertise I used to race a plastic slider over the top of a Ziploc bag, getting my daughter's school sandwich out the door with maximum efficiency. There were joys to being a young mother, but now that my child is a mother herself and my youth is long gone, I have discovered my truth: the hard fronds of the waves, these white palms, are my paradise.

Plastic Surgeon, Australia

The anxieties are always different. This patient is nervous about his waist and thighs. In half an hour I'll be removing a few pounds of excess fat. Last week I explained the procedures. 'You should do it now,' I said, 'the skin gets less elastic as you age. Enjoy the best body you can in your youth, *carpe diem*.' The young man nodded; I was preaching to the earthly choir. I turned to the X-ray for relief. The body is always more interesting when seen this way, when the bones, surrounded by a light haze of muscle, appear dazzling. My secretary makes fun of my Catholic leanings, but truly it does look celestial. 'Right,' I said to the young man, 'here is what we will do.' It was a relief to speak to him in such a detached way, after the small talk of the first few minutes. I can never get used to it; I always feel as if I am interrogating the patient, since the questions only go one way. He seemed eager to talk about himself, and his life in the big city, Adelaide. For me conversation is like the magazines in the waiting room, a way to pass the time. The waiting room is identical to all of the other waiting rooms in the country. The magazines are the same too, full of the same glossy pages about the royal wedding of Charles and Diana, the launch of a Russian spacecraft, tips for better skin and nails, pastes for a brighter smile.

'You can come in now,' I told him, gesturing and hurrying back to the surgery with my clipboard. The man has dark hair and blue eyes. When he set down his magazine, it splayed open to a page featuring an advertisement for rum, with heavily-tanned blonde youths relaxing on the beach. All of them were perfectly shaped; even the palm tree they leaned against had no excess leaves or branches. Now the man is in the surgery, and I am preparing my little trimming tools, my modern shears and loppers to nip away his excess mass. By any natural standard, there isn't much. Yesterday I passed a gardener at work on a palm, on the path I take every day to my office. 'You and I are in the same business,' I scowled. He laughed. He knows my name, the infamous moments of bile that others link to my talent, and also the good salary that I make, the best one in town. 'Give me a discount, Doc,' he said, rubbing his belly and the plump trunk of the palm before him. Now, it occurs to me as I go in with the vacuum suction, I'm not even sure it was a joke.

The translator works to create the luminous. She works to draw out the radiance of the material as she moves between periods of time, between languages. She soothes and coaxes as a healer or priestess. The greatest translator, of course, is History. Time does not move in a progressive way; rather, all moments touch and communicate as a gleaming network of roots beneath a forest which it is possible to sense, even as we help to compose it.

Tree Designer, Argentina

Riding the bus this morning on my usual route by way of the shopping district, a thrill ran through me. The holiday season has almost begun. It's only September but the window dressers are enthusiastic, and have already pulled out Santa mannequins to accompany the latest clothing line. But Santa isn't in the typical red suit of the North, his belted, red-suited, jiggling paunch sticking out over loose trousers. No, our Santa wears tight flowery swim trunks. I can't even imagine fluttering snowflakes or crunchy white crystals under my boots at this time of year, since for me the holidays are a period of warmth and sunshine. The months also bring a spike in work, always a good thing. I design trees for rich clients, which keeps me occupied the whole year round, but to decorate a Christmas tree is special. My clients tend to look for something new and bold. I've gone wild with trimmings; I've added smartly-dressed angels and bright bows; I've shaved the tree half-bald for a punk musician; I've flirted with the risqué and the innocent. Once I delivered a tree inside a cake to a *quinceañera* birthday party, and at the height of the madness, instead of a dancing lady, out popped the conifer. Another time I hung a tree from the ceiling upside-down. My notebooks are full of sketches, and everything sparks my imagination. I studied costume design, but trees are better-behaved subjects than people. They have personalities, too. Seeing the Santa reminded me of where I am. After all, this isn't a country of pines. What if I were to change the variety of tree from pine to palm? Dark green would shift to a lighter hue; I'd get to work with leafier boughs. I could burst fireworks above it, or spin its spiky crown like a top, or tie little rings to the ends of its leaves, or turn the coconuts into glittering ornaments. I could wind a ribbon up the trunk, or make it into a maypole. Maybe, in this part of the world, the palm tree will become the real symbol of Christmas for the masses, and open up a whole new market for my business. How many families can afford an imported pine, anyway? The palm is the tree that by all rights belongs next to surfer Santa and his towelled reindeer.

Partygoer, Spain

At Café Zurich, the gentleman drinks a cigaló with brandy. 'It's not very strong,' he complains to the waiter, who laughs, because the man is singing out his grievance from the top of a table.

The police arrive at the Rambla to throw out a man selling magic colored flying balls from the middle of the walkway. But he escapes by throwing the ball into the air, and disappearing with it.

Palm trees that line one side of the street debate the Catalonian independence movement with palm trees that line the other.

The white rabbit observes the festivities in the plaza. Every year he is deflated and reinflated as part of the Bon Nadal. Every year in his hatch he dreams about the smell of chestnuts and pine.

'O happy day,' sings the leader of the gospel group before the Christmas public. A tourist is looking for 'Hospedaje' after the festivities, but in her fatigue this 'O happy day' sounds the same, and she feels that she has a home to celebrate.

Guru, New York

I arrived with very little plan. All I sought was to convert the sick masses to a better way, the way that I had learned from my own teacher. This, I knew, required patience. I had come from afar to a land where people filled the space of religion with false gods, versions of yoga that I did not recognize, false mysticism. I set up my practice in a place that didn't look promising, and in the beginning, no one came. And then they did start to show up, first a few and then many. I found myself inventing ways to fill the time, with cooking, chants, studies of the ancient books and prayers to my master, whose framed pictures cover the same walls that were so bare when I got here. Physical location isn't important, I know. But the healthy detachment that I cultivate finds its greatest challenge when I remember my little hometown. What I most recall are the palms of my native land, and I thought that it would be nice to hang a poster to show them. I couldn't find a single one that replicated what I remember, however. The form was there, but the essence was missing. Most of the posters seemed to have been designed for the dormitories of college students, and featured a pop style, green silhouettes or parodies of tropical beaches. They were not the palms that I knew and loved, ragged and tired yet noble.

My practice grew, and I was content. I took pleasure in supporting my disciples and writing angry newspaper articles about the imitation faith of my detractors. But the lack of palms made me unhappy. One day I went for a stroll, mired in a kind of nostalgia that I do not like to admit. Instead of walking around the downtown, as I usually did, I decided to wander along the waterfront of Battery Park, looking toward Ellis Island. Here I felt more like a stranger; here I felt the pleasant outsiderness that I had experienced when I first arrived, when I had been closer in time to my palm trees. My feet carried me along the shore for miles, until at last they grew too heavy to go on. I sat down on a bench and looked up. And then I saw her, my palm. There she was, in the tired yet noble green metal of the Statue of Liberty, the great palm of New York City.

Where thought has opened up one cell of reality, it should, without violence by the subject, penetrate the next. It proves its relation to the object as soon as other objects crystallize around it. In the light that it casts on its chosen substance, others begin to glow.

Adorno, Minima Moralia
trans. E.F.N. Jephcott

I turned to books of all kinds, manuals brimming with instructions, paths to perfection, bricks to construct the interior castle. All of these guides counseled different strategies, yet as I moved my finger over the words, I found that their elliptical reckonings gloried too much in the conceptual. I needed an image. I looked out the window and there it was, an ordinary and scraggly tree, so common and even ugly. But wasn't this also a face of existence? Couldn't this too be an object of devotion, not profane although perhaps prosaic? The image was at hand. I could draw it toward my heart for contemplation. And then it was that another phrase sprang to mind, unbidden: for a heart in peace, every village is a celebration. I will speak of many villages, I thought, many places to which I have never been. Many others like myself whose lives have been touched, albeit ever so lightly, by the presence of this tree.

Passenger, India

We were late, but he stopped to buy marigolds. Incandescent yellow, the soft petals were joyful embers against the dashboard black. *We were late, but he stopped to buy marigolds.* A boy handed them through the window, along with the tiny hard bud of a perfect rose, bright pink, a drop of water running down its side. I couldn't stop looking; it held my gaze, as I repeated the invented words in my head. *We were late, but he stopped to buy marigolds.* We'd almost ruined the car in a pothole as the driver attempted to bypass roadwork. Afraid of a puncture or loss of air, he had all four tires filled with a long thin tube. This was the first detour. *We were late, but he stopped to buy marigolds.* The flowers were the second. The dust was thick, the sun strong, and motorcycles zipped by us in the wrong direction past sleepy palms and chai-sipping shop owners. We were late, but he stopped to buy marigolds. We would nearly miss our flight to Udaipur, and next to me the others were tapping their feet on an imaginary accelerator. But before we knew it, he slid the car again to the side of the road. *We were late, but he stopped to buy marigolds.* There was a red mark on his forehead, and his shirt was the color of the flower garland he wound about the gold Om frame, a picture card inside it. We were alive. Nothing else mattered so much as to give thanks. *We were late, but he stopped to buy marigolds.*

'The nuns are moving to another convent,' says my friend. Her aunt is one of these nuns, and has entrusted her with taking care of the now-empty convent in San Miguel, on the outskirts of Santiago.

This part of the city has a slower form of life; it's almost a town, and in the streets elderly couples sell eggs and other things to eat from the counttryside. Here in the convent, beneath the grape trellis where fruits hang crystalline and green, a chimera of clusters frozen in this heat, we read a novel out loud, in a round of five: an act of speaking and intimate listening.

We get through the book in about an hour, silently noting its patterns in the way that we happen to read similar sections every time (one: letters, two: the perspective of a boy, three: brutal political facts, four: anecdotes from school, five: memories), which speaks to how the author structured her narrative, although it seems magic. The dogs run frenetic through the garden's swaying palms as slowly it darkens.

We try not to think of the possible rats out there, as under the trellis, in the candlelight, the convent reveals its purpose: the creation of a pleasant space that is joined to nature, not as an innocent Eden but as a self-reflective closeness to one's inner life and to life with others, the communion between which might, perhaps, be called God.

Cyclist, Chile (II)

Like a butterfly flying off a marble column, I think. I'm cycling through Plaza Dignidad, ex-Italia. A policeman is watching the people go by. No doubt he knows what they think of him. His whole body is protected by a shield, a helmet, heavy clothes. Then up flutters his hand, the only visible part of him, to direct traffic. A miracle, this hand of his, a butterfly that wishes to escape.

I rush through, my helmet hanging from the handlebars. It's illegal, dead wrong, but the day holds such freshness. Sun, breeze, trembling nets of shadow in the splendor of summer: I want to feel all of it on my skin. The trees burn green, and delicate leaves pattern the ground. Under the pavement, the palms. This intoxication of the delicate holds such possibility. My gathered-up hair is a spiky palm, molded to no heavy helmet.

From the oasis of the lanes I career into the dry wasteland of the plaza. Even this has its charm. Does the policeman know the feeling of being exposed to the elements? The generous quality of being out in the open, wind-stripped, laid bare, naked of excess protection? Disclosing one's being to fine slips, hard trips, occasional lapses of taste, frequent errors? But also to unexpected beauties, the surprise of a fresh self-respect? Does he know something of these subtle failures and triumphs, or for him is everything simply order, rule of law without distinction, the architecture of all or nothing?

With the plastic barrier of his protective gear, gun in holster and stick in hand, he looks so hard, with no inner life, none of the tree's vital impulses to shed and split, peel and grow. There he is, in a vain attempt to preserve his Rome. But then up goes his hand, fluttering just so, in a wish to escape. Like a butterfly flying off a marble column.

As I sit under the lamplight, I feel happy. I laugh, I talk to myself, I talk to the books. I talk to the trees, and in my mind the palms form a swaying jungle of stories. I shimmy up one trunk after another and listen to the secrets they whisper. In the darkness of my room, the blue glass of the lamp after I replace the wick turns into a lantern which I use to navigate the forest. I see into the great cycles of growth, death and rebirth, and see how the palm stands as one firm possible trunk, one instrument that can encompass the problematic labyrinths of dominion, desire, domesticity and devotion. I see, too, that I am neither alone, nor the first one to think of such things, that this Book of Palms has an ancestor, many ancestors. Together all of us form part of a hidden, luminous process, as souls born and reborn into different bodies, experiencing suffering and joy, cruelty and laughter in mythical time. And now I will set aside the lantern of my explanations, to dwell in the stories which give off a soft glow of their own.

Jessica Sequeira has published the novel *A Furious Oyster* (Dostoyevsky Wannabe), the collection of stories *Rhombus and Oval* (What Books), and the collection of essays *Other Paradises: Poetic Approaches to Thinking in a Technological Age* (Zero). She is also an active translator of poetry and prose by Latin American authors, both contemporaries as well as figures such as Winétt de Rokha, Sara Gallardo and Teresa Wilms Montt, whose playful imaginations remain vital. Currently she lives between Santiago (Chile) and Cambridge (UK), where she is writing a PhD at the Centre of Latin American Studies on literary exchanges between Latin America and India.

Sublunary Editions is a small, independent press based in Seattle, Washington. It publishes short books of innovative writing from a worldwide cadre of authors, past and present. Subscriptions are available at:

subeds.com/subscribe

OTHER SUBLUNARY EDITIONS TITLES

Falstaff: Apotheosis
Pierre Senges (translated by Jacob Siefring)

926 Years
Kyle Coma-Thompson, Tristan Foster

Corpses
Vik Shirley

The Wreck of the Large Glass / Paleódromo
Mónica Belevan

Under the Sign of the Labyrinth
Christina Tudor-Sideri